A FRIGHTFUL CASE OF MURDER IN THE FASHION STORE

AN EMILY CHERRY COZY MYSTERY

DONNA DOYLE

PUREREAD.COM

Publisher's Note: This is a work of fiction. Names, characters, places, and incidents are a product of the author's imagination. Locales and public names are sometimes used for atmospheric purposes. Any resemblance to actual people, living or dead, or to businesses, companies, events, institutions, or locales is completely coincidental.

CONTENTS

DEAR READER, GET READY FOR ANOTHER GREAT COZY...

READY TO SOLVE THE MYSTERY?

Elderly sleuth Emily is shocked when she realizes that murder is the new fashion in Little Oakley!

But could a clothing sale truly be good enough to die for?

Turn the page and let's find out...

1

"What do you think of this one?" Emily Cherry plucked a bright green skirt with a matching blouse off the rack and held it up in front of her. Dress for Success was full of clothes, but she was having a hard time deciding if any of them were right for her.

Anita made a face, the corners of her mouth reaching down toward her jawline. "No, dear. That's terrible with your hair. And you know I love your hair, but it's a bit much."

"I'm not sure the color is quite right for the office, anyway," Emily agreed as she put it back on the rack and moved on, searching for something else.

"I don't know why you're agreeing to go back there." Anita pulled a sleek black pantsuit off the rack, checked the price tag, and put it back. "I mean, you said after your stint at Pierce's Auto Shop that you were done trying to go back to work."

Emily shrugged as she considered a pair of slacks. "I know, but this is Phoenix Insurance. I worked there for years, and I imagine it'll be like riding a bicycle. I've already done it all before, so it'll be much easier. It's still just a temporary job for a couple of weeks while one of their newer people is out for carpal tunnel surgery, so it's not as though I'm completely heading back into the work force."

"And you don't have anything suitable to wear? You traded in all your work clothes for denims and joggers?" Anita teased as she moved over to a rack of jewelry.

"I might as well have," Emily laughed as she patted her hand on her hips. "I think I might've gained a little bit of weight over Christmas or something."

"Haven't we all?"

"Oh, stop. You look as fit and fashionable as ever. Now help me find something that will say I'm ready to go to work, but I'm not desperate for their paycheck." The two of them shared a laugh as they moved over to the next rack.

"How are you ladies doing today? My name is Valerie. Can I help you ladies find anything?" A slim young woman came up next to them, her big brown eyes eager as she watched them. Her hands seemed to move automatically as she fiddled with necklaces and tucked price tags into collars, keeping the store looking as neat and straight as possible.

"I'm not sure," Emily admitted, already feeling a little bit defeated even though this was the first store they'd tried. "I've got to get some business attire, and I don't really know what I like anymore. This top is kind of cute, though it's a bit expensive."

Valerie's smile widened a bit as she raised an eyebrow. "That's going to be part of our sale that's starting at the end of the week, if you'd like to come back for it."

"Oh." Emily tipped her head as she considered the shirt a little bit longer. It really was more than she wanted to pay, and there was no need to spend too much money when she was only going to be at Phoenix Insurance for a couple of weeks. "I just might do that. I'm going to need to find something soon, though."

"If you're looking for something on a budget, we do have a clearance rack right over here." Valerie guided them to a space closer to the back of the store. "Can I go ahead and open up a fitting room for you?"

"Not just yet," Emily replied. "I want to look around a bit more before I really start deciding. Thank you, though."

"Of course. Just let me know if you need anything." With a sweet smile and a nod, Valerie headed up toward the front.

"My goodness," Anita noted quietly as she poked an elbow into Emily's ribs. "A young shop clerk who's actually helpful! You don't see that very often anymore."

"That's true enough," Emily agreed. It made her appreciate the fact that they'd decided to stay right here in town to shop. They wouldn't have had the same experience if they'd gone to a bigger city.

A plain gray door that led to the stock room opened up, and a tall, thin man emerged. His hair was cropped a bit too short around the back, emphasizing his long neck. Emily watched as he marched straight up toward the front of the store, looking furious as he stepped around behind the counter.

"Valerie," he said sternly as he stepped up next to the register. "We've got to talk about what you're doing."

The girl looked up from the tag she was affixing to a pair of earrings. "I already double-checked these in the system, and they should be on the clearance rack," she explained.

"Not that! I mean when you're ringing up customers!" The man gestured angrily toward the register.

"I'm not sure what you're talking about, Peter." Valerie finished with the earrings and set them aside.

"You're putting your employee number in for every sale instead of asking who helped the customer," Peter explained through gritted teeth. "You can't do that. We have a strict policy here at Dress for Success of giving credit for the sale to whoever actually assisted the customer out on the floor. It's the only fair way to do it, since that part of the job takes a lot more time than just ringing up an order."

Emily knew that none of this was her business, but the store was just too small for her not to hear. She kept an ear tuned to the conversation as she flicked through the clearance rack.

Though he was clearly the manager and much older than her, Valerie didn't look intimidated by the conversation. She shook her head gently. "I understand our policy, and that's exactly what I do. If I've helped the customer, I put in my number. If Brianna has helped them, I put in hers."

Now Peter pointed one long finger at the register. "Then explain to me why there are so many of them in your name, when the two of you girls work the same number of hours every week!"

She pressed her lips together for just a moment but kept her cool. "I think you might want to talk to Brianna about that. I take this job very seriously, and I do my best to help every customer who comes in here when I'm working. I greet them. I take the time to ask them what they're looking for and guide them to the right rack. I get them in the fitting room, and I'm always making recommendations for shoes and bags that will go with their outfits."

"Right, just like you're supposed to do," Peter retorted sarcastically. "That still doesn't explain why there are so many transactions in your name. I'd fire you if I didn't think your crazy aunt would come back and try to get some sort of revenge on me for it. Just make sure you're putting Brianna's number in when you should be."

Valerie nodded. "Of course. Just like always."

The manager stormed back into the stock room just as another salesgirl came out of it. She sidestepped him quickly and spotted Emily and Anita at the clearance rack. "Do you ladies need any help finding anything?"

Emily noted the nametag and discovered that this was the Brianna who was just being discussed. She surmised that Brianna and Peter must've just been having a conversation in the office about who was making what sales. "I think we're all right for now. I'm just going to get a couple of things and come back for the sale on Friday."

"That's going to be a good one." Brianna had dark hair that she'd pulled up into a bun, and it was a nice contrast to her bright blue eyes. "I'm going to be picking up quite a few items for myself during that sale, and I think quite a few other people in town are going to be doing the same thing."

"Hmm." Emily looked again at the blouse that she'd been considering earlier. "I might have to try to get here early, then."

Brianna turned so that her back was to the cash register, where Valerie was working through the rest of the earrings. "I was planning to come in about thirty minutes before our official opening time that day, if you want to duck in and grab what you want before everyone else does."

Emily opened her mouth, not sure what to say, but Anita answered for her. "She'll be here."

"Are you making my schedule for me now?" Emily asked, teasing her best friend.

"Only when you need me to," Anita replied with a smile. "You need those clothes, and if someone doesn't make you come back in here and get them, then you'll never do it yourself. Now then, I think we've looked through every single piece for sale in here. Let's see what you've got so far."

2

"You're the pushiest salesperson I know," Emily said with a smile as she carried her bags out of Dress for Success and turned toward her car.

Anita grabbed her by the arm and turned her back around, pointing across the street. "And I'm not done yet. If we're already here, then we might as well see what they have at To the Nines. The two tops you've picked up so far aren't going to get you through a couple of weeks' worth of work, and you haven't even tried them on. You may end up returning them."

"Oh, I don't know."

"Let's just see," Anita encouraged. "We never know until we go find out."

Emily smiled and shook her head. Anita had always been the bolder one of the two of them, ready to step out into an adventure or to tell someone just what she thought of them. Emily was working on being a little bit more like that, although she knew she'd never be quite that forward. "That's your personal slogan, isn't it?"

"I think it should be," Anita said with an approving nod.

To the Nines was very similar to Dress for Success right across the street. It was a small shop that didn't offer quite the same selection as the big department stores, but it was enough to be grateful for in a small town like this. Trendy music pumped a little bit too loudly through the space as a woman with thin brown hair came around the counter and practically ambushed them. Her nametag denoted her as Melissa.

"Hi, there! We're here to help you dress to the nines! What can I help you with?" Her dark eyes glanced from Emily to Anita and back again eagerly.

Emily waved vaguely at the merchandise. "I think we're just going to take a look around, thank you."

The clerk scowled down at the bag in Emily's hands. "I've seen you've already been to Dress for Success."

"That's right," Anita confirmed with a bob of her head. "And we'll be going back at the end of the week for their big sale."

Emily wasn't so sure that they needed to explain all that, since it was obvious that this girl was just as desperate for sales as Valerie and Brianna across the street must be. "I'm just looking for some work clothes."

"Then you definitely don't want to go back over there," Melissa sneered, lifting her chin in the air to indicate Dress for Success. "It's a terrible place to shop."

"I have to say that I agree," said a woman who'd been lingering over on the other side of the register, near the formalwear. She sashayed over in a gray skirt suit that fit her like a second skin, even though she had to be well into her fifties at the very least. Emily supposed the black gloves and the wide-brimmed hat that she'd paired with it must be the latest fashion, but she certainly didn't know.

"Yes, you won't find anything you want over there," the woman continued, casting a dirty glance across the street. "It's not easy to find all the right clothing. I would certainly recommend shopping here."

Melissa jumped a little at the woman's recommendation and then beamed. "Thank you very much."

"Of course." The woman looked Emily up and down, clucked her tongue, and left.

"There you have it," Melissa chirped, practically bathing in the afterglow. "I'm sure you can see there's no point in going back to Dress for Success."

Anita, not the kind of person who appreciated being told what to do, straightened her shoulders. "I don't think so.

The staff was very helpful, and we found some good bargains."

"You only think you did." Melissa glanced down at the bag again, clearly wishing she could see what was inside of it. "They always claim that they're having great sales, but they're really not much better than what our regular prices are. Not to mention the fact that their clothing is terrible quality. As soon as you put anything through the wash once, it's going to fall apart."

"My dear, you might want to find a way to make your store sound good instead of trying to make another store sound bad," Anita advised as she brushed past Melissa and swooped into the racks of clothing.

Emily followed her. "You're probably going to make that poor girl cry, you know."

"I doubt that." Anita moved past the casual wear and began swiping jackets aside as she looked for the perfect outfit. "She's one of those people who thinks she's better than everyone else and knows more than they do. It doesn't exactly make me want to buy anything."

"I can't say the clothing makes me want to get my charge card out, either," Emily agreed as she noted the missing button on a blouse. "Do you see a clearance rack?"

"How are we doing, ladies?" Melissa had pounced on them once again, emerging from behind a display of dresses and noting their empty hands. "What sort of work clothes would you like? Maybe a nice skirt suit?"

"I think something a little bit more casual," Emily began to explain.

"Oh, like this." Melissa was at her side now, even closer to her than Anita was, grabbing items off the rack and piling them in Emily's arms. "This color would be great on you, and you'll really love the way this fabric drapes. Try this one. I know it doesn't look all that great on the rack, but it's much better once you have it on. How do you feel about houndstooth?"

Emily blinked at the armful of clothing she now held, feeling as though she'd hardly even had a chance to see what the items were before Melissa put them there. "I really just wanted to look around, that's all."

"We've got some other errands we need to run, anyway." Anita scooped the numerous items out of Emily's arms and handed them back to Melissa before guiding Emily back to the front of the store. "Thank you anyway!"

When they were out on the street, Emily felt like she'd just been holding her breath underwater and had finally been able to break the surface again. "That was overwhelming!"

"Like I said, she really needs to change her demeanor if she wants to sell some clothes. At least now we know that To the Nines doesn't have clothing or salespeople that we're interested in dealing with." They moved back across the street so they could work their way back toward Emily's car.

"Did you get a chance to talk to Peter?" A tall, lanky young man with shaggy blonde hair stood in front of Dress for Success, talking to Brianna. He wore a black t-shirt with a big logo that resembled a dinner plate. Emily recognized it as being from The Dish, a local diner.

The salesgirl fluttered her hands. "I tried, but I don't think it did any good."

"You told him you needed more hours, right?" the young man insisted.

"Sure, but he said there's not much point in giving me those hours if I'm not making any sales. I tried to tell him that Valerie was stealing all the credit, and he went and yelled at her for a bit, but of course he didn't really do anything about it." Brianna folded her arms in front of her chest and leaned against the building where she'd be just out of sight for anyone inside Dress for Success. "He seemed more interested in berating me for how poorly I've been doing."

"I need that money, Bri," the young man insisted. "You've got to do something."

"I'm trying, okay?"

Anita clucked her tongue against the roof of her mouth as soon as they were out of hearing range. "Young people these days sure are dramatic. We all start out with money problems, and it takes a long time to work through them."

"Someone doesn't have money problems," Emily noted as they passed a long, dark car. A driver waited behind the wheel, reading a newspaper and looking bored. If there was anyone in the back, Emily couldn't tell. The windows were tinted such a dark shade that they might as well have been just as solid as the rest of the car. "Who in Little Oakley would have a vehicle like that?"

"Maybe it's someone from out of town," Anita suggested.

"Can you just imagine?" Emily paused to dig her keys out of her purse. "Some celebrity coming down from London to shop in Little Oakley on the chance that they won't be recognized?"

Anita laughed as she got in the passenger seat. "If they've done that, then I'd like to see them get bossed around over at To the Nines by that Melissa girl. She can tell them just how to spend their money." She lifted her chin in the air and narrowed her eyes in her best impersonation of Melissa. "Don't even bother going to Paris or Milan! They charge way too much for their clothes, and you can get everything you need right here!"

"You're terrible!" Emily started up the car and checked for traffic. "I'll just have to look in my closet and see what I can squeeze into, and then I'll go back to Dress for Success for that sale. It'll be good enough for now."

3

"Does this look all right?" Emily turned around to show off her outfit.

Rosemary, sitting on the edge of the bed, looked up at Emily with her big gold eyes. She tipped her head slightly to the side and then proceeded to bathe her whiskers.

"Too boring? Well, that'll just have to do since it's for work, anyway." Emily turned back to the dresser to find the earrings and necklace she wanted. "I do feel bad about leaving you, but we've done this once already. I think you're going to be just fine, and it's only temporary."

The cat was too busy trying to slick her whiskers back down to bother with any input. She licked her paw and smoothed it down her cheek, but the wild white strands insisted on curling and twisting every which way.

"I'll be bringing you with me, in my own way." Emily picked up the small, framed photo of Rosemary off her dresser. "I'll have you right there on my desk. How does that sound?"

Rosemary sniffed the corner of the picture frame and purred.

"That's my girl. You be good, and wish me luck!"

The drive to Phoenix Insurance wasn't a long one, and it was a route Emily felt she could do with her eyes closed. She'd made this commute more times than she could recall when she'd worked here full time, and she liked the familiarity of it. That was exactly why she'd agreed to come back, after all. It would only take a day or so to get herself reacquainted with everything, and then it'd be just like she was at her old job again.

She felt a small pang of sadness as she pulled into the parking lot. Her dear Sebastian had worked here with her, and he'd been gone for a couple of years now. Though they hadn't always worked the same hours and they weren't even in the same part of the building, it'd been kind of fun to know that they could have lunch dates together or that they might pass each other in the hall. She still missed him terribly, even after all this time.

"No point in getting yourself down," she reminded herself as she turned off the engine and checked her hair in the mirror. "Just go in and remember all the good times you've always had here."

With a smile on her face and a bit of excitement fluttering in her chest, Emily strode through the front door. The little vestibule hadn't changed a bit, with a potted fern on either side of the front door. It was plain and simple, but that was just how she liked it.

As soon as she stepped through the inner doors, however, Emily realized that even though the same ferns were there to greet her, nobody else was. There had once been a single receptionist's desk right at the front of the building. Though a few different people had filled the position in Emily's years there, it was their job to direct customers to the department or person they were needing. That desk still sat there, but all the other walls on the main floor had been taken down to reveal numerous workspaces. There were desks off to themselves, and yet others were grouped together. Work areas with a table in the center and comfortable chairs surrounding them had been set up closer to the windows. Instead of the bland gray colors she was expecting, the office space embraced the blazing orange and red of the Phoenix Insurance Logo here and there with upholstery and rugs that were difficult to look at.

"I'm more than happy to help you," the woman at the front desk said.

Emily smiled and stepped forward. "My name is Emily Cherry. I'm the new temp, although I suppose you could really say I'm the old temp since I—"

She paused as the other woman held a finger up and then gestured to the headset in her ear, which Emily hadn't noticed before. Emily clamped her mouth shut, embarrassed. She enjoyed her own headset when she was at home and trying to crochet while she talked on the phone, but this setup seemed guaranteed to embarrass someone.

Finally, the woman tapped the button on her headset and beamed at Emily. "What can I do for you, ma'am?"

Emily thought about giving her an earful, but she knew it was just her own pride that was hurt, and the girl was just doing her job. "I'm the new temp," she explained simply.

"I see. I'll get Alexis for you."

A woman who was probably younger than Emily's own children stepped out of an office near the back. "I'm Alexis, the general manager. It's nice to meet you. Is something wrong?"

"I'm sorry. I guess I was expecting that Mr. Miller still worked here," Emily explained. "When HR called and asked about me coming to work temporarily, I thought the recommendation would be from him."

"Oh, no," Alexis said with a shake of her head. "He retired last year, actually. We worked with a temp agency for a while when we needed someone to fill in, but we didn't have much luck with them. That's when we decided to check through former employee records, figuring it would be a good way to find people who knew the job. Here's where you'll be working."

"I see. That makes some sense," Emily replied hesitantly. She looked down at the stark desk. It was grouped together with a few other ones, but she was used to working by herself in a cubicle. "This is very different."

"It's a hybrid office layout that allows for all different types of work to be done in the spaces that are most appropriate for them. Most of what you'll do can be achieved right here, and you'll have other employees nearby who can help you if you need it. If you're on the phone with a client, you can take one of the private desks over there. The tables, chairs, and couches make good conference areas when you have a customer you need to speak with in person," Alexis explained. She pointed at the computer monitor. "I take it you remember how to use all the software?"

Emily grimaced. She had learned quite a bit about her laptop ever since she'd started blogging, far more than she ever thought she would. But this wasn't blogging. "I'm afraid much of what we did when I was working here was still on paper."

"Don't worry. Hunter here can get you started. If you have any questions, feel free to ask any of us." Alexis left Emily in the care of Hunter, who was typing away rapidly on his computer.

Sitting down, Emily got out her little photo of Rosemary and put it right next to the monitor where she'd be able to see it almost constantly. She was going to need to see that sweet little face on a very frequent basis to make it through the next couple of weeks.

After several hours of trudging through the software, asking Hunter and anyone else a million questions, and generally feeling like she was completely incompetent at something she used to know like the back of her hand, Emily found herself at one of the tables with a client. She was perfectly aware that she was only doing this because everyone else was busy, but she was determined to do the best she could. "Hi, I'm Emily. What can I do for you?"

"I'm Erica. It's nice to meet you. I came in because I just don't know how I'm going to pay our insurance bill this month. You see, my husband's hours have been cut back. I stay at home because our children are still very young, and most of the jobs I could get pay less than what we'd have to shell out for daycare. I just don't know what I'm going to do." Erica's eyes welled up with tears.

"There, now." Emily might not know how all the fancy computer systems worked, and she certainly wasn't used to the strange layout of the office, but counseling people on their finances was a talent that she'd naturally built up during the course of her time at Phoenix Insurance. She fetched a box of tissues, a piece of paper, and a pencil. "I'll have to have someone else take a look at your account to see what options are available for your bill, but I'm sure I can help you with more than just that. Let's talk about your income and your bills and see what we can cut out, shall we?"

4

"You should have seen how happy she was when she left," Emily gushed. She sat at her kitchen table with her favorite pen, writing away. "I forgot that was my favorite part about working there. Other than working with Sebastian, of course. But there's something incredibly satisfying about going through someone's finances with a fine-toothed comb and seeing where they can cut out some bills or bring in some extra income. I think Erica was very happy by the time she left."

Rosemary sat on the chair next to her, patiently listening to Emily's recounting of her first day. Her big gold eyes were fixed on her owner's face as though she was truly captivated.

"You humor me," Emily pointed out as she turned back to the list she was making. "I do admit that I did have to refer her to someone else so that she could get her questions about her account answered. I'm starting to learn their software, but my old brain just doesn't take to that sort of thing as quickly as I would hope. Or perhaps as quickly as they hoped, either."

The cat leaned over and bumped her head against Emily's elbow.

"I appreciate the compliment. It's all right, though, because going to back to Phoenix has given me some fantastic ideas for a blog. I know all kinds of things about budgeting and saving money, and that's the only reason that I'm doing as well as I am right now. This job isn't going to leave me a lot of time to write the articles, but I figured I can at least get the ideas down. I can post about creating a household budget, reducing home energy costs, buying the right amount of insurance, and how best to take advantage of sales. Speaking of sales..." Emily glanced at the clock and jumped up from the table, startling Rosemary. "I'm sorry, my dear. I've got to get going. Brianna offered to open up the store early for me, and I'd feel pretty bad about it if I didn't bother to show up. I'll see you this evening, and I promise we'll have some time together. Goodbye!"

Emily rushed out the door and headed downtown. She was going to get to Dress for Success just on time. Both Melissa and that strange customer at To the Nines didn't seem to think very much of the other store or their sales, but Emily wasn't sure she thought so much of them, either. There was plenty of room for both stores and their styles, even in a small town like Little Oakley.

As she headed for the shop, however, she saw that traffic was nearly at a standstill. "What's going on?" she mused aloud as she bobbed from one side to the other, trying to see around the clog to figure out what was happening. "Did they decide to resurface the road right during rush hour?"

There really wasn't time to figure it out, and so Emily pulled over into the nearest parking space. At the rate traffic was going, it'd be just as fast—or faster—if she walked. She stepped out onto the pavement and marched toward Dress for Success, hoping some of those tops she'd been admiring weren't already sold out by other excited patrons who'd been told about the sale.

As she neared the shop, however, Emily saw that traffic wasn't being held up by an accident or construction crews. Emergency vehicles, their lights flashing every which way, had piled up in the street right in front of Dress for Success. Police tape flapped in the breeze as it made a large rectangle that extended the entire length of the building and stretched out almost to the street. Police in black uniforms and bright yellow vests stood out in the misty morning as they moved throughout the scene.

Emily knew she should probably head back to her car, cut through an alley, and get out of this part of town so that the police could do what they needed to do, and others could get to work. Her curiosity, however, quickly got the best of her. It took a much firmer hold when she spotted a familiar face among the uniforms. "Alyssa! Dare I ask what happened? Was it a break in? Someone could've just waited for the sale to start," she chuckled.

But the young detective constable looked grim as she turned to face Emily. "I wish it were something as simple as that. I'm afraid one of the employees has been killed."

The blood instantly drained from Emily's face. "That's terrible. How? I mean, I was just in there the other day and chatting a bit with the girls who work here."

Alyssa glanced over her shoulder before taking Emily by the elbow and leading her away from the front doors a bit, where the senior officers had converged. "In that case, I can refer to you as a potential witness and we can talk about this, if you don't mind."

Though she was shocked, Emily understood exactly what Alyssa was doing. The young woman wasn't really supposed to discuss her cases with Emily, but the two of them tended to work well together. "That would be fine."

"Did you know a Brianna Hughes?" Alyssa asked, her pen at the ready above her notepad.

"I would assume that's the same Brianna I spoke to in here," Emily replied, finding her throat a bit dry. "I needed some work clothes, and my friend Anita and I went shopping."

Alyssa nodded. "And did you notice anything unusual? Anything that might explain why someone would want to kill her?"

"My goodness, no. Not that I can think of. I'm sorry. I think my brain is a little cloudy this early in the morning. Let's see." She tapped her finger on her chin, trying to recall more than the simple fact that she'd been in the shop. "Her manager, Peter was his name, was rather harsh. He told the other girl here that he wanted to fire her, and he seemed rather agitated. Oh, yes, and I understand there was a bit of a confrontation between Peter and Brianna about her work performance. He's the first person I'd be looking at."

Alyssa's hand moved quickly as she jotted this all down. "He's already arrived, actually. He came to open the store and was the one who found Brianna. We've had a chance to speak with him. He's got an alibi, but of course we'll have to check it out and make sure it's solid."

"I see. I'd make sure he's telling you the truth, whatever it is," Emily advised. "There was something I just didn't like about him."

"I know that feeling," Alyssa sympathized. "I wish I were allowed to go with it a little bit more, but the department wants hard evidence instead of emotions. I'll be looking into him, though. Anything else?"

"That's all I can really think of for the moment. It was an odd day." Emily shook her head and clucked her tongue. "Such a shame."

"Bradley!" someone shouted.

"I've got to go. If you think of anything, just call me." Alyssa gave Emily's arm a friendly squeeze before she ducked under the police tape and trotted over to her superior.

Emily stood there for a moment, staring at the building. It'd seemed like just a normal clothing store when she'd been in there the other day, a place that she'd imagined would've pretty much remained the same from week to week if something like this hadn't happened. The bright signs in the windows cheerily advertised the sale that was supposed to start today, but nobody would be buying anything.

5

Emily, however, *did* still need to buy something. She'd waited for this sale before she finished out her work wardrobe, and she wasn't going to have anything to wear to work that day if she didn't do something about it. Her original plan had been to pick up an outfit or two and wear one of them out of the store, but now it was all falling apart.

However, there was still another clothing store in Little Oakley, and it was right across the street. Emily threaded through the slowly moving traffic toward To the Nines.

Melissa was standing there at the front door, and she held it open as Emily walked in. "What happened?"

"What?" Emily hadn't liked Melissa much when she'd met her in here a couple of days ago. The woman had been pushy, rude, and snobby. Emily had expected much the same attitude out of her today, but Melissa seemed subdued, or maybe even shocked.

"I saw you talking with one of the detectives," Melissa said as she pointed across the street and chewed her lip. "I was wondering if you knew what happened over there."

Emily hesitated. "You don't?"

"No." Melissa's eyes were glued on the scene across the street, taking in every bit of it. "I park in the alley behind the building, and I come in through the back door. I didn't even realize something was going on until I came out front to unlock the door and turn the lights on, and then I saw all the emergency vehicles.

She wasn't supposed to just give out information that the police had yet to release publicly, but considering that the coroner's van was making its way through the traffic across the street, she knew there was at least a little bit she could share. "Someone has been killed."

"It was Brianna, wasn't it?" Melissa asked instantly.

Already thrown off by the news itself, Emily braced her hand against the counter. "How did you know?"

Melissa finally turned away from the front windows and widened her eyes as she stared at Emily. "You mean I'm right? It really is her?"

Emily nodded. She forced herself to move over to the nearest clothing rack. She did, after all, have to get to work shortly. She hardly even saw the clothes in front of her, though, thinking only about Brianna. When had it happened? Who would do such a thing? Would Peter have a solid alibi? "I'm afraid so."

Melissa sighed heavily. "She had a way of getting herself mixed up in the wrong kind of business."

Forcing herself to pick out a couple of outfits, Emily draped them over her arm. "I take it you knew her?"

Melissa went behind the cash register and leaned her elbows on the counter. She studied the way the light reflected off her nail polish. "I did, but not recently. She used to work here up until about six months ago."

"Is that so?" Emily realized she hadn't even looked at the price tag. It went against her own personal budgeting rules to just buy something at full price and without really thinking about it, but right now she was desperate for clothes and information.

"Yes. Can I get you a fitting room?"

"That would be lovely, dear." Emily followed Melissa to the back of the store, where she unlocked a louvered door. "Thank you. I'll probably wear these out of the store if I decide I like them. I've got to get to work today. Now tell me, why did Brianna leave?"

She could hear Melissa fiddling with her keys just outside. "She wanted better pay."

Emily had never been a big fan of trying on clothes. The lighting in the dressing room was never right, or she was wearing the wrong shoes, or the tags got in the way. As a result, she'd learned to go through the process as quickly as possible to get it over with. "That seems reasonable enough."

"Hmph. Maybe."

"Could you get me this top in gray instead of black?" Emily asked, hanging the blouse in question over the top of the door.

"Certainly." Melissa had much better customer service when she was subdued, Emily noted. She returned quickly, having already taken it off the hanger for her.

Emily pulled it on and turned in the mirror. It wasn't quite her style, and she knew there were clothes she'd have preferred at Dress for Success, but that was obviously out of the question. It would just have to be good enough. "If you don't mind my saying so, you don't seem to have liked Brianna very much."

Another sigh came through the door. "I guess you could say that."

There was obviously a lot on Melissa's mind, but she was being hesitant to say it out loud. That struck Emily as odd considering how eager Melissa had been just a couple of days ago to discredit her competitor. "I mean, it certainly sounded like you don't like anyone at Dress for Success very much. I know my friend was a little short with you when we were in here before, but I have to admit I was very curious as to what was wrong with the place. If they're doing something I don't like, then I might not want to give them my business."

Hangers rattled. "It's not really the store itself."

"Oh, so then the staff? Well, that could be just as bad." Emily ran her fingers through her hair, but her wild curls were going to do what they wanted regardless of what she thought. She stepped out of the fitting room in her new outfit, with her old clothes under her arm. "I'll take it."

Melissa guided her up to the register. "It might have been just fine that Brianna wanted to get more pay, but I think she was also slipping money from the till. I just couldn't prove it."

"Oh, my." Emily took the bag Melissa offered her to put her other clothes in. "That certainly put you in an interesting position when she needed a reference."

"You're not kidding." Melissa punched the buttons on the cash register far harder than was necessary. "And then she goes over there to Dress for Success, and I'm pretty sure she was giving her new manager all the inside information on how and when we run our sales."

It had taken a little bit of work to crack her open, but now Emily could see that Melissa was ready to let all of her frustrations out. She swiped her card through the machine. "My goodness. That's not very fair."

"I know! And now I've lost tons of business, and I can't afford to have too many sales or else I won't make enough money to keep the doors open!" Melissa ripped the receipt off the register and handed it over.

"You're probably going to get quite a few more customers, now that Dress for Success has all of that going on." Emily barely glanced across the street, not wanting to look at all the flashing lights and vehicles any more than she had to. It was a sad situation, even if Brianna had done the things Melissa accused her of. In fact, Emily wouldn't have been surprised if Melissa herself was the murderer that the police would soon be tracking down. "You mentioned that Brianna often got mixed up in things she shouldn't. Who do you think did this?"

Melissa was angrily tapping her nails on the counter, but now she snapped her head up. "Probably that no-good boyfriend of hers, Jonah. I don't know him well, but I've seen him around. He's hard to miss considering that the two of them would come right out onto the pavement to argue."

While the discussion Emily had witnessed between Brianna and her boyfriend hadn't exactly been an argument, it was definitely a conversation that most people would've had privately instead of in front of a downtown business. She had to wonder if Melissa wasn't the only one on the suspect list that was already starting to form in her mind. “I hope not.”

“I’m sure the police will figure it out.” Melissa looked over her shoulder and out the window, but then she quickly turned away.

Emily couldn’t blame her for that, no matter how she felt about Brianna. “Thank you for the outfit, dear.”

Melissa wasn’t really paying attention. She was now chewing on her thumbnail as she stared at the wall across the room. “Mmhmm. All sales are final. Have a nice day.”

6

The Daydream Café was jam-packed with the work crowd, and Emily felt proud to be a part of it. "What do you think of this? Your mother back in her dress shoes again, getting a paycheck like a regular person."

"I think you should stay at home with your cat," Nathan advised.

"Oh, poo!" Emily reached across the table and gave him a playful slap on the arm. "You're always raining on my parade. The weather around here does enough of that for the both of us, you know."

"I do, but I also know that you were said you were done working after the last time." He finished off his sandwich and reached for his napkin.

Emily bobbed her head from side to side. "Yes, yes. I know. That's what Anita pointed out as well."

"Because it's true!"

"Yes," Emily conceded, "but that doesn't mean a woman can't change her mind. Besides, I really thought this would be different."

He leveled those dark blue eyes of his at her. "And is it?"

"Yes. Just not the kind of different I was hoping for." She waited while he signaled the waiter for a check. "I'm glad to be getting out there in the world and helping people. I've assisted a young woman in putting her household budget back to rights, and I've spoken with several other people about how to improve their finances."

Nathan nodded approvingly. "That sounds right up your alley from what I remember."

Emily had to agree. "It is, and it's given me wonderful inspiration for my blog. When I find the time to get back to it, that is. But I just wish that things around the office hadn't changed so much. Most of the people are different. The way things are done is different. Even the furniture is different! It doesn't feel like going back to an old job at all, but more like a completely new one."

"There's nothing saying you have to stay," her son pointed out.

"Certainly there is! I said I would, and that's all it takes." Emily checked her watch. "Oh, you're going to be late for your meeting."

"Let me just get this paid for and I'll walk you to your car," Nathan offered as he pulled his wallet out.

"No need, dear. I can make it down the street on my own. Thank you for lunch." Emily kissed him on the cheek and headed outside.

The spring day was bright and beautiful, the sort of day that made her wish she really did have some time off so she could work out in the garden or take her grandchildren to the park. That wouldn't be happening today, but it was likely that the spring weather would still be around when she was done working for Phoenix. She'd just have to wait.

As she headed toward her car, she couldn't help but glance down the street at Dress for Success. The yellow police tape had been taken down, and the sign in the door announced that they were open. Emily checked for traffic and made her way over there. She still had a little bit of time before her lunch break was over, after all.

The big bright sales signs were still up in the window, but the inside of the store felt incredibly subdued. There was no music playing, and nobody was at the front to greet her. Emily glanced around, feeling like she shouldn't even have been in there. She knew what'd happened there, and even though there was no physical evidence of any sort of altercation, the very air felt thick and heavy.

Valerie came out of the back office. She startled as she looked up at Emily. "Oh, I'm sorry. I didn't hear you come in."

"That's all right, dear." Emily rubbed her fingers along the strap of her purse nervously. It was probably a mistake to be here, but her curiosity had gotten the better of her. Now that she stood in front of Valerie, who's dark eyes were somber and rimmed with red, she was starting to question herself. "I saw that you were open and thought I'd stop in. Are you doing all right after…everything?"

Valerie lifted a shoulder and let it fall as she fiddled with the necklace and dress on a mannequin. "I suppose so. Well enough, anyway. It's very stressful to be in here, knowing what happened. Or rather, not knowing what happened. That might make it worse. It's very difficult to be here."

"I'm sure that's true," Emily sympathized. It was difficult even for her to be here, and it was only for a few minutes. Poor Valerie seemed so upset, but there were many questions still bouncing around in Emily's brain. "Were you and Brianna close?"

"Not exactly." Valerie took a belt from a nearby display and added it to the waist of the dress, cinching it in the middle and completely changing the look. "She was always upset with me because I do well here. I get a lot of sales, but it's because I was always trying harder. I wanted to be as successful at this job as I could possibly be instead of just standing around and gathering my hourly wage simply for existing. It was a difference in who we are as people."

"I'm sure that made it very difficult for the two of you to get along." Could Valerie possibly have been the murderer? Emily knew that Brianna had tried to get her coworker in trouble for claiming so many sales in the register, and Valerie certainly knew the store and the schedule well enough to make it happen. There was something soft and sweet about her, though, and Emily had a hard time imagining her actually killing someone.

"Very much so," Valerie agreed. She stood back to look at her work for a moment before selecting a pair of shoes from a wall rack. "It was always tough when Brianna was here, but now that she's gone it's simply exhausting. I think I'd quit if I had a choice, but I need this job while I work my way through school."

"Oh, what are you going to school for?" Knowing this wouldn't likely get Emily any of the clues she truly desired, but she'd taken a liking to Valerie and was genuinely interested.

A small smile made its way onto the girl's lips. "Fashion. I've always had a passion for it. Even when I was little and playing with my dolls, the clothes from the store were never good enough. I wanted to make my own, and I learned to sew at a very young age for just that reason."

"How wonderful! I can't say that I'm any good at fashion myself," Emily admitted. "I like to blame this awful red hair of mine since it clashes with everything, but I think there might be more to it than just that."

Valerie tipped her head a little as she studied Emily's hair, and then she reached for a nearby rack. "Actually, something in a deep green like this emerald blazer would look lovely with your hair and really make it stand out in the best way."

"Oh. Do you think so?" Emily eyed the gorgeous jacket. "I usually just go for black or gray."

"Deep, bold colors would be so much more flattering." A bit of the light had come back into Valerie's eyes as she fetched a cobalt blue dress. "Something like this. Or I have it in purple, if you'd like to try it. It would be lovely."

"The fabric is very nice," Emily admitted, wondering if maybe there was something to what Valerie was saying. "I like the idea of bright colors, but I'm always so worried it'll be too much."

Valerie nodded. "It doesn't suit every occasion. This champagne shade would make everything look soft and warm, and your hair would give the overall effect of a little bit of blush or pink. Beautiful." She held up a beaded tunic.

"You're quite good at this." It was such a flattering experience that Emily thought she'd buy everything in the store that Valerie pointed to.

"I'm trying to be, and that's why I'm in this program," Valerie admitted. "Actually, part of the program is that I have to design and create several outfits to be presented in front of a panel of judges. That's the final step before I can move onto an internship, and it's coming up next week. Would you be willing to model for me?"

"What?" Emily lost her grip on the beaded tunic and nearly dropped it. "Me? But I'm just an old lady. Nobody would want to see me in a fashion show!"

Valerie gave her a serious look. "I know that's how things have been in the past, but I'd really like to change it. Everyone deserves a chance to look good, no matter their age, size, or coloring. You have wonderful skin and beautiful hair, and I'd love to bring it all out. I can't pay you, but you'd be able to keep the outfit I made for you."

"Well, all right," Emily agreed, feeling her cheeks brighten. "I suppose I could do that."

"Wonderful! It's been hard to get people to agree to this, and you'll be helping me out so much!" Valerie clasped her hands under her chin, her eyes shining brightly.

The door to the stock room slammed open and Peter emerged. "Well, I'm officially cleared!" he announced as he strode through the sales floor, typing away on his cell phone. “I just had yet another interview with the police, but they finally figured out that I told them the truth. Of course, they wouldn’t believe me until they found security footage showing that I was getting home right at the time of Brianna’s death, but at least it means I didn’t have to find a lawyer. Like I could afford one on what I make here.”

Valerie, looking horrified, cleared her throat. “I’ll have to talk to you about that later, sir. I’m with a customer at the moment.”

Peter straightened, his thumbs finally still as he gaped at Emily. “Oh. Um, sorry. Carry on.” He turned on his heel and went back into the stock room.

“I’m sorry about that.” The light in Valerie’s eyes had once again been extinguished.

Emily patted her arm, wishing there were something she could do to make things better. “That’s all right. I’ll try on a few of these, and you can tell me what you think.”

7

"Didn't you just have lunch with Nathan yesterday?"

"I did. What of it?"

Anita swung around the corner of the street, sending Emily teetering toward the passenger window. "I just know that you usually stick to only a few meals out a week so that you don't go over your precious budget."

"Is there something wrong with my budget?" Emily put her nose in the air, but she brought it back down again as Anita hunted for a parking spot, getting a little too close to the bumpers of the other cars along the street.

"Not at all, but it certainly makes me wonder. Either they're paying you far more money than they ever used to at Phoenix, or you're so miserable there that you're desperate for companionship on your breaks." Anita yanked on the wheel and jerked the car into an available slot. "Or perhaps the most likely thing going on is that this lunch has something to do with that young woman's murder."

Emily knew perfectly well that Anita didn't have a problem with her budget. She also knew that Anita understood her better than anyone else. "It might."

"All right. Tell me. I at least want to go in prepared." Anita pulled her lipstick out of her purse and touched up in the mirror."

"Do you remember when we came out of To the Nines and Brianna was talking to her boyfriend on the sidewalk?" Emily asked.

Anita rubbed her lips together and flipped up the mirror. "Right. The ones with money problems."

"Yes. That was her boyfriend, Jonah. I only know this because Brianna used to work at To the Nines, and the lady in there told me Jonah was the first person she'd suspect. She didn't give me a whole lot of reason for that, other than the fact that the two of them had a lot of rather public arguments. Well, that and Jonah can't keep a job, but I don't think that makes someone a murderer. Anyway, I remember that Jonah was wearing a shirt from the restaurant that day."

"Which is why we're here," Anita concluded, looking up at the big logo of a dinner plate above The Dish.

"Precisely. The police have already cleared Peter, the manager at Dress for Success. Now it's time to move on to my next suspect." Emily hated that someone had died, but she definitely loved trying to figure out what happened.

"And what if he works in the back washing up?" Anita challenged. "Are you going to claim you can't pay your bill and offer to go work back there too, just so you get a chance to talk to him?"

Emily laughed. "Have a little more faith, Anita! Either he'll be here, or he won't, but we'll get to share a meal whichever way it goes."

They chose a table near the middle of the room, where they'd have a chance to see everything happening around them. The little diner was busy with the lunch crowd looking for a quick bite, ordering burgers and fries, chicken sandwiches, or club sandwiches. The air was thick with grease, and old timey music blared from a jukebox in the corner.

Anita raised an eyebrow at the menu but didn't complain about it. "So, how are things at Phoenix Insurance, anyway? Is it still just as great as you remember it?"

"Not exactly. I suppose I haven't had much of a chance to tell you about it yet, have I?" Emily was just about to launch into everything that'd changed about her old workplace when their waiter arrived.

"What can I get for you ladies?"

Emily blinked. The young man was wearing a black t-shirt with The Dish's logo on it, just as anyone else who worked here would be. He was tall and lanky, and his blonde hair was threatening to grow down over his eyes if he didn't get it cut soon. 'Jonah' was boldly printed on his nametag. She'd hoped to run into Jonah here, but she didn't think it would be quite that easy. In fact, it'd happened so quickly that she wasn't quite prepared. "I think we'll need just a few more minutes, please."

"What are you going to do?" Anita whispered when he'd left. "Order a hot dog and then ask him if he murdered his girlfriend?"

"I'm sure I'll find a much better way of doing it than that." Emily's eyes skimmed the menu, but she wasn't really reading it at this point. "I just feel so bad for him. He looks just as miserable as Valerie does."

Anita shook her head. "The other shop girl?"

"Right, which reminds me that I have quite a bit to tell you about my little chat with her." Emily was nervous about the idea of the fashion show, even more nervous than trying to track down a killer. The latter was something she was getting used to, but parading around in front of a panel of judges while wearing a custom-made outfit? That was new!

Jonah made his return soon enough. "Did you ladies decide what you wanted?"

Emily looked up at him. They were in the middle of a busy restaurant, and it was difficult to tell how she should approach this problem. Anita was right; she couldn't just come right out and ask him if he killed his girlfriend. That wasn't how Emily usually managed to get information out of people, anyway. "I think I've seen you before. Brianna was your girlfriend, wasn't she?" Emily asked gently.

His chin crushed in with dimples as he pressed his lips together and blinked away his tears. "She was," he managed to choke out.

"I heard what happened, and I'm so sorry," Emily replied sincerely. She really did hate this for him. He'd suffered a great loss, and he was already back at work. "Perhaps I should introduce myself. I'm Emily Cherry, and this is my friend Anita. I didn't know Brianna all that well, but you have my most sincere condolences."

"Yes, from both of us," Anita chimed in.

His eyebrows scrunched together. Despite how tall he was, Jonah looked like a little child who'd just lost his puppy. "It's nice to meet you. And thank you. I appreciate it."

"Of course. I just wish there were something I could do to help. I'm sure the two of you had a lot of plans together." It was hard to know exactly how to show her sympathy when she'd only met Brianna briefly and had merely seen Jonah on the street. They were young, though, and it stood to reason that they probably had big dreams and ideas for their future together.

Jonah gripped his pencil tightly and scribbled on the corner of his notepad. "Yeah, we did. It wasn't like we were going to be able to go through on any of them, though."

"Why is that, dear?" Emily felt terrible for asking him these questions, but she knew it was the only way she was ever going to get to the bottom of this case. Melissa had seemed so sure that Jonah was the culprit. Would he be this upset if he were the one who'd killed her? Wouldn't it have made more sense for him to leave town? More so, she wasn't sure what his motive would've been.

"Well, money," he said with a roll of his shoulder that suggested it should be obvious. "We wanted to save up and get a place together, but I was already behind on rent from when I changed jobs. We knew we'd have to get that caught up before any other landlord would rent to us, but my boss wouldn't give me any more hours. People have been skimpy with their tips lately, too."

Emily nodded. "Yes, I certainly know there are a lot of folks trying to save up their money. Was Brianna trying to make more money?" There was no telling what sort of scheme the girl could've gotten caught up in if she was looking for extra cash.

"She wanted to, but it was pretty much impossible." Jonah now tapped his pencil eraser against his thumb. "She couldn't get any more hours, and this other girl she worked with was always hogging all the commission for herself."

"Oh my." Emily had to hide the fact that she already knew Valerie, Brianna, and Peter had been disputing over who should be getting commission and how.

"Yeah. It was like neither one of us could get ahead no matter how hard we tried. Luck's just not on our side, and it's not as though either of us had a rich aunt to support us like Valerie does." Someone at another table signaled to him, and he held up a finger and nodded. "Sorry. I've been talking about this way too much, and I'd better get back to work. Did you know what you want to eat?"

Emily and Anita put their orders in quickly and then waited until he walked off to the other table.

"Well, that was certainly interesting," Anita noted.

"I agree." Emily drummed her fingers on the table. "He's upset enough over Brianna's death that I don't think he'd be here if he didn't have to be. You heard that he's behind on rent, and I'm sure the last thing he needs right now is to get evicted."

"So where does that leave you going next?" Anita asked, obviously a little more intrigued now that she'd gotten involved.

Emily shook her head. "I'm not sure, at least not yet. Did you hear him mention that Valerie has a rich aunt?"

"I did, and I wish that I'd had one at some point. When my aunt Lucy died, she only left me a shelf of romance novels," Anita cracked.

"But it sounds as though Valerie has a rich aunt right now, and it must be someone who supports her in some way," Emily noted. "When I was talking to her at the store yesterday, she said she *needed* the job while she worked her way through fashion school. Why would someone need a job like that if they had a wealthy aunt who could help them with it?"

"Maybe the aunt doesn't like her," Anita offered, "or the aunt isn't as wealthy as everyone thinks she is. The way young people are these days, maybe Valerie even made the aunt up just to make herself sound better."

All of those were possibilities, but Emily knew she'd probably get a chance to find out. First, she'd be leaving a rather large tip for their waiter. "Did I tell you I'm going to be in a fashion show?"

8

Back at her new temporary job, Emily held a piece of paper in her hand that'd become very familiar by this point. She'd looked at it so many times since she'd found it at home. It never should've been in her home in the first place, considering it was a Phoenix Insurance claim form for Dorris Financial Consultants. Emily had wanted to believe that it'd accidentally gotten mixed up in some other papers, because she knew Sebastian would never go against company police and bring important documents home when they were supposed to be in the client file at the office. However, there was no mistaking the number five written in Sebastian's very own handwriting at the top of the page, followed by a question mark. Emily had yet to figure out if there was any significance to that particular document, but now that she had the chance, she knew it needed to be put back where it belonged.

The problem was that she couldn't seem to figure out where it belonged. Though most of the information on clients was now in the computer, there was still a large bank of filing cabinets in the back room for the few things that they still needed real signatures on. Emily had gone straight to the drawer where the folder for Dorris Financial should've been, but it wasn't there. She'd checked several places, thinking perhaps it'd been misfiled, but to no avail.

"Hunter?" She turned to the young man who worked at the desk next to hers.

Hunter seemed to be very dedicated to his work. He'd made a few small bits of polite conversation with her here and there, but for the most part he was either on the phone, typing away at his computer, or working directly with a client. He certainly didn't slack off. "Hm?" he asked without taking his hands off the keyboard or slowing down his typing.

"I found this form lingering in the bottom of the drawer, and I need to put it up," she explained. It was a lie, and she felt guilty for it. Emily didn't like to think of herself as a liar at all, but if she told anyone the truth about finding the claim form among Sebastian's things, then it would make him look bad. She couldn't stand that thought, not when he wasn't even around to defend himself. "I couldn't find the file for it. It's for Dorris Financial."

"Dorris Financial?" he repeated, finally stopping and turning around. He narrowed his eyes at the form. "The name isn't familiar. How old is that?"

"Hmm." She pretended to scan the form for the date, even though she knew exactly where it was. Emily had looked over this paper numerous times since she'd found it, and she'd been familiar with this kind of form when she'd worked here. "Looks to be about three years old."

"Wow. Someone really let that slip through the cracks," Hunter noted. "I don't think they do business with us anymore, so the file has probably been shipped to an off-site storage facility."

"Really?" Emily didn't know if she should be more surprised that one of the biggest clients Phoenix Insurance had during her time here had left them or that they'd done so much business they could no longer keep all the paperwork inside the building.

"Yeah." Hunter handed the form back. "You might want to go check with admin on the other side of the building. They can probably tell you where to find the file."

"I'll do that, thank you." Emily knew her main function here was to be available for customers, but now that she'd already started this little adventure, she couldn't just stop. She headed over to the administration offices. This part of the building, tucked away from the public, was where all the little things were taken care of, such as human resources, tech help, training, and building management.

She paused for a moment as she gazed across the sea of desks that'd once been a maze of offices. Apparently they liked the more open floorplan here, too. She found a small sign on the front of a desk that said, 'Records.' That certainly looked like the right place to start.

"Excuse me," she said as she walked up to the desk. "I can't find the appropriate file for this document, and I was told I should check with you in case it's being store off-site."

A man who looked to be in his mid-forties, with a balding pate and a stomach that bumped up against the edge of his desk even when he leaned back, took the form and peered at it through his glasses. "I would imagine you can't! We haven't done business with Dorris Financial in a while. Where did this come from?"

She waved vaguely toward the side of the building she'd come from. "I found it in a drawer. I remember the name from when I used to work here. I'm just filling in as a temp right now."

"Hm. That's some sloppy filing, if this can slip through the cracks for that long. Yep, as I recall they started having some major family problems a couple of years ago. I don't know exactly what it was, but they could no longer pay their bill. I think the whole company ended up shutting down. I'll have to get this over to the storage facility sometime, but don't worry. I'll get it taken care of."

"Thank you very much." Emily turned to leave, but she stopped at the water cooler. As the cold liquid ran down her throat, she had to wonder what this all meant, if it meant anything at all. Why did Sebastian have that claim form? Why did Dorris go under? She didn't even remember reading anything in the paper about it, but then again that was right around the same time that Sebastian had died. Half of the world could've slid off into the ocean and she wouldn't have noticed.

Back at her desk, Emily worked away the afternoon. She was just getting ready to leave when the secretary paged her. "You've got a call on line five."

Pleasantly surprised that anyone would be asking for her directly, Emily picked up the line. "This is Emily. How can I help you?"

"Emily. This is Jonah." The voice on the other end of the line was breathless, desperate.

Her brain churned for a moment before the name clicked into place. "Jonah. Forgive me for saying so, but I'm surprised to hear from you."

"I'm sorry to reach you at work. I had heard you and your friend talking about your office when you were at the diner. I just—I just didn't know who else to call. Or what to do. I—I don't know."

"Slow down, Jonah. It's all right. I don't mind that you called me here. Now what's going on?" She pressed the phone harder against her ear as though that would help her hear better.

He pulled in a deep breath that sounded like static against the receiver when he blew it out again. "I was just shaken down behind The Dish by this big guy. He was a real rough looking type. You know, the kind that's probably spent some time in prison. He pushed me up against the wall in the alley and told me I'd better shut up if I knew what was good for me."

"Oh my." Emily spread her fingers over her collarbone. She'd taken a liking to Jonah in the short time that she'd talked to him, and this didn't sound good. "Are you hurt?"

"No, not beyond a bruise or two. It was just so weird. I don't know what I did, and he wouldn't tell me. He just wanted to threaten me."

Emily turned slightly away from Hunter so he'd have less of a chance of overhearing her conversation, even though he was already on the other line. "Did you tell the police?"

"No way," Jonah replied instantly. "They already questioned me from top to bottom about Brianna's death, and it's obvious they don't like me. They're not going to take me seriously if I bring this to them. I'm sorry to burden you with this. I don't have anyone else to call, and I thought since you knew Brianna that maybe you'd have some idea."

She clamped her teeth together. The poor boy had been ostracized so much that he was quicker to turn to some old lady who'd chatted with him in a restaurant than anyone else. Emily knew she had to do something, but she didn't quite know what. "Do you think this had anything to do with her death?"

"Maybe. The only other thing the guy said was that he 'wouldn't want to upset the store owner,' whatever that means. I know Brianna had gotten in it with her boss Peter, but he technically wasn't the owner of Dress for Success. Listen to me. I'm babbling now."

"No, Jonah," Emily said softly. "You're just fine. I happen to know someone on the police force, and I can pass this information along and see if there's anything they can do with it."

"Really? Thank you, Emily. I felt like kind of a fool for bringing this to you, but maybe it wasn't such a bad thing." He genuinely sounded relieved.

Emily was glad, but she knew the struggle wasn't anywhere close to being over. "I'm glad. You just make sure you keep yourself safe, okay?"

"I will."

When they got off the phone, Emily was glad it was the end of the day. There was no way she could concentrate on work at this point. Who had threatened Jonah? And who was this store owner the guy had referred to? Considering the way Melissa had acted, she certainly hadn't been crossed off the list of suspects yet. Emily knew exactly where she'd be going after work.

Her cell phone jangled as she fought the afternoon traffic. "Hello?"

"Emily, it's Alyssa."

Any other time, Emily would've been glad to hear from her. She truly considered Alyssa to be a good friend, and she had some interesting information to pass along. But she could hear the tension in the young officer's voice. "What's wrong?"

"Nothing, or at least nothing that *should* be wrong. A man has been arrested for Brianna's murder," Alyssa informed her.

"Oh, good." If it was the same man who'd terrorized Jonah, then he wouldn't have anything to worry about.

"It should be good, but I'm not sure it is. He was brought in based on his fingerprints," Alyssa continued. "The problem is that he has this high-powered attorney who will probably bail him out with a snap of his fingers, and then I imagine he'll get him off without a problem. That is, if he was even the guy who did it."

"You don't think it was?" Emily hit the brakes as traffic slowed.

Alyssa sighed. "There are just too many things that don't line up. This guy is a nobody, and he had no ties to Brianna. We usually find some sort of connection with a murder, some real motive instead of just a random decision to take someone's life. This guy has also only ever worked menial jobs, so he shouldn't be able to afford a hotshot lawyer like this."

"Could he be an old school chum doing him a favor?" Emily suggested. She, too, suspected there was more to it than that, but she liked to know every angle was being covered.

"It's not outside the realm of possibility, but I don't know."

"Can you tell me who it is?" Emily pressed.

"I'd probably better not do that right now," Alyssa said quietly.

"I understand." As enthralled as she was on this case, Emily didn't want to get her in trouble. "I do have some information for you, though."

"I plan to swing by To the Nines," Emily explained when she was done relaying her conversation with Jonah to Alyssa. "I want to see what Melissa is up to, and if there's anything I missed before."

"I'm not sure I like that idea, but I can't exactly stop you from going shopping. Just be careful," Alyssa advised.

Emily flipped on her turn signal. "I will."

9

It was already getting dark outside by the time Emily found a space for her car and then walked up the street. She'd been rehearsing this visit with Melissa ever since she'd gotten off the phone with Alyssa, but she still didn't know exactly what she would say. She knew Melissa had to have something to do with Brianna's death. It simply made sense, and yet the woman didn't really seem like a killer. If she got lucky, she'd at least have more information to pass along to the police.

While she hadn't been sure what to expect when she arrived at To the Nines, it certainly hadn't been finding Melissa standing out in front of the store with a suitcase in her hands.

"Are you closing early?" Emily asked innocently as she walked up, hoping to catch her before she left.

"You could say that." Melissa's hands shook as she fiddled with a ring of keys, trying to find the right one. Her hair, which had been carefully combed before, was frizzy as though she'd run her fingers through it multiple times. Even her clothes looked rumpled, which definitely wasn't a good look for someone who proclaimed to run the best boutique in town.

"That's such a shame. I was hoping to come back and pick up a few things." In truth, Emily had more than enough clothes now that she'd bought an armful from Valerie. The deep, bold colors were a nice change for her, and she was enjoying them very much. What better excuse did she have for coming back to To the Nines than to shop, though?

"I'm sorry. It'll just have to wait, I'm afraid." Melissa put the key in the lock, but she didn't turn it. She just stood there, staring in the windows at the dark interior of the store where the racks of clothing stood waiting. "I put a lot into this place, you know."

"I would imagine so. It's never easy to run a small business, and certainly not in a small town." Emily looked Melissa over carefully. The young woman didn't look as though she'd been injured at all, but something had definitely happened. Had she received a visit from the rough guy who had also frightened Jonah? Or what if Melissa and this other mystery man were in cahoots together, and something had gone wrong? Every idea Emily had only seemed to lead to more questions.

Melissa nodded as she reached out and turned the key firmly in the lock. "I guess it doesn't matter now."

"Of course it does," Emily insisted, laying a hand on her arm. "You're not just closing the place up, are you?"

"I don't know what choice I have. I mean, I never thought she'd actually kill her. It was all about the program, I thought. I mean, that was it. It was simple enough, but now everything is out of hand and I'm the one who's feeling guilty about it all." She was babbling now, her eyes wide as she gazed down at the pavement.

"Honey, if there's something going on, then I can help you," Emily promised. "How about you and I walk down to Daydream Café? I think they're still open. I can get you a nice cup of coffee and something to eat, and we can talk."

Melissa glanced down the street, and the glare of the lights seemed to wake her back up. Pure terror was written on her face. "I can't. I've got to go. This is so much more than I ever signed up for. I thought it was just innocent, no real victim. But I was so wrong."

"Melissa, please," Emily begged. She sensed that she was so close to the truth, but it was slipping through her fingers like water. "I don't quite know what's going wrong, but I can help you. I know people, very nice people, who will listen."

"No. I'm sorry." Melissa shoved her keys in her pocket and took a tight hold on the battered suitcase. "I've got to get out of here. Please, don't tell anyone you saw me." Without a backward glance, Melissa slipped down the alley between the buildings and disappeared into the darkness.

"Melissa!" Emily called, but it was no use. She was gone.

Emily felt a chill run up her spine as she turned back toward her car. That hadn't gone according to plan at all. She didn't really have any more information, and one person whom she'd been sure was involved was now probably going to leave town. She'd call Alyssa and tell her, in case they wanted to track her down, but she had a feeling that the young woman had already melted into the night.

Turning her collar up against the late evening chill that even the spring weather hadn't quite been able to drive away yet, Emily started thinking. Melissa had mentioned a program, and she'd also referred to the killer as a female. Was it possible that Valerie was the killer after all?

10

"There. Perfect." Valerie made the final adjustments to the deep blue knee-length dress and the matching jacket. It was trimmed in black and fit Emily like a glove. "Are you ready?"

Emily's breath was shaking. In fact, every part of her was shaking. "I've never done anything like this before. I hope I do all right for you. I know you have a lot riding on this."

Valerie beamed at her sweetly. "Don't you worry about that. Nobody expects you to do anything more than what we already talked about. And they're judging the outfit, not you. Even if they were, you look fantastic if I do say so myself."

"And I feel it," Emily replied honestly as she glanced in the mirror that'd been set up backstage. Valerie had already helped her find some wonderful outfits at Dress for Success but having something custom made to fit her body was the most amazing experience! Never had she put on clothes that made her look better.

Checking her watch, Valerie turned toward the stage. "It's time to start. I'll see you out there."

Emily waited just behind the curtain with several other women behind her. There hadn't been much time to introduce herself to the rest of Valerie's models, but she could tell that all the clothes had been put together with the same careful hand. She peeked out onto the stage.

"Hello. My name is Valerie Ferguson. I'm delighted to be presenting my items to you today. First up, we have Ms. Emily Cherry."

That was her cue. Emily didn't think she could move, but her feet had other ideas. She stepped out from behind the curtain and strode toward center stage, just as Valerie had instructed her. She was vaguely aware that Valerie was describing the outfit she wore and why she designed it, but Emily hardly even heard her. She was too focused on the sheer number of people who'd shown up. There was the row of five judges right in the front, which she'd expected. The first several rows of the auditorium seating were also filled, however. Emily realized these must be the other students in the program, plus their models and anyone else who'd shown up to support them. She hoped the smile she'd pasted on was still there as she slowly spun around and headed toward the other side of the stage, where she was to wait near the back so all the models would eventually be available for the judges to see.

When it was time for the next model, a woman who must've been Valerie's age wearing a brightly colored dress with lots of layers and movement, Emily felt as though she could relax a little bit. The worst of it was over, and the judges had more to look at than just her.

It wasn't over for Valerie, though, because when all the outfits had been paraded across the stage, it was time for her interview. "Thank you so very much for taking your time to view my creations," she said with a smile when the last model had crossed the stage. "I'm happy to answer any questions you may have."

A slim woman with a severe face and glasses perched halfway down her nose leaned forward. "Please, Miss Ferguson, tell us what your goal was here with these designs."

Valerie was ready for this one. "I believe that fashion these days so often caters to the wealthy, the fit, and the young. My hope was to create a diverse range of items that would look good on anyone, because we all deserve to feel beautiful.

A man who had been writing in a notebook the entire time and was still writing was next. "Our program strives to ensure that students get a full understanding of all aspects of the fashion industry, and so we require experience in retail. Please, tell us what you came to learn while working at Dress for Success."

Ah, so that was why she said she needed her job there! It didn't necessarily have anything to do with money at all, but it was a condition of the program. There was one part of the mystery solved anyway, even if it wasn't the part Emily had been most concerned about.

Valerie cleared her throat, and though Emily couldn't see her face at the moment, she could tell she was having a hard time. "It's been an interesting journey, certainly. I can see that selling clothes, regardless of the price or the designer, is about making the customer feel good. It's about helping them make choices that they can be confident about even after they get home and they're in different lighting and looking in different mirrors. It's not about how many sales you make, but how many people you make happy."

The man raised his eyebrows in appreciation as he continued to scribble notes.

The next judge was a woman in her thirties who sat back with one arm folded across her chest while she nibbled on the earpiece of a pair of glasses that she obviously didn't need. Her cheekbones looked like they could slice through a roast, and she kept her eyes narrowed on Valerie instead of her designs. "Miss Ferguson, this next question is perhaps a bit personal, but we've never shied away from that sort of thing here. I believe we all know that your aunt is Minnie Ferguson, a very generous donor to our school. In fact, she's here today. Let's all give her a round of applause for all that she's done."

Emily noted Valerie's shoulders stiffen before she gazed out over the audience and spotted the woman in the second row who stood up and gave a dignified little wave. She'd seen her before. That was the pompous woman she'd run into at To the Nines, the one who'd agreed with Melissa that nobody should be shopping across the street and who had openly disdained Emily's outfit. If that were the rich aunt that Jonah had referred to, and if she wanted Valerie to get through fashion design school, then why would she be shopping anywhere other than Dress for Success?

"Now then," the judge continued, "my question for you is this: You went to a lot of trouble to get through this program. There are rigorous classes, a job requirement, a massive portfolio design, as well as this show and interview tonight. Tell me why you worked that hard instead of just asking your aunt to make another one of her generous donations that would guarantee your internship?"

Valerie folded her hands on the podium in front of her. She looked out in the audience at her aunt and then back at the judges. "You're correct in that my aunt has been very generous. She contributes to numerous organizations in the community, and she has been kind enough to take care of me ever since my parents died. But

I wanted to prove, both to myself and to the panel before me today, that I could do this without any kind of assistance. I wanted to know that I not only wanted to but deserved to be a part of the fashion world, not because of whom I happen to be related to, but because of my talent, passion, and hard work."

Another thundering round of applause went through the building.

"Thank you very much, Miss Ferguson."

That was it. The whole thing had been short, as Valerie had promised, but Emily felt as though she'd lived an entire month in those few minutes. She and the other models headed backstage and straight for a break area that'd been set up for them with cold bottles of water and snacks.

"Can you believe that?" the young woman in the brightly colored dress said as she cracked open a bottle of water. "Poor Valerie can't get credit for her work no matter what she does, because Aunt Minnie is always around to steal the show!"

Emily glanced over her shoulder to make sure neither Valerie nor Aunt Minnie were around to hear, but she saw only the next presenter and her gaggle of models making last minute adjustments to their clothing. "Is this something that happens a lot?"

"Oh, yeah." The girl appreciatively smoothed the fabric of her dress. "It might look like that woman is generous with her money, but she only throws it around when she knows it'll get her what she wants. She's incredibly strict, and Valerie has spent her whole life trying to please her."

"That had to be very hard on her, and especially after losing her parents." It seemed that Emily was learning an awful lot about Valerie today. There was still a chance that she was the one who'd murdered Brianna, but after spending all morning with her, Emily really didn't think so. A wealthy orphan who was smart and spirited enough to make her dreams come true didn't strike her as the kind who would murder an annoying coworker. "Although it seems as though she's doing just fine on her own."

"Finally," the girl agreed. "Aunt Minnie has manipulated plenty of other people in her life before. Once, when she was just a kid, Minnie threw Val a birthday party and *paid* a dozen other children to show up. It sounds like a kindness on the surface, but Val was absolutely devastated to know they didn't want to be there for her. It's no wonder she was so determined to do this on her own."

"And to know that it was truly her own accomplishment," Emily murmured. She glanced toward the curtain, but Valerie was nowhere to be seen. The poor girl had been through a lot. Did that make her a more likely suspect?

11

A short time later, Emily stepped out the side door of the building and moved around toward the front to head toward the parking lot. She almost didn't see the slim figure leaning against the brick near the front doors as she passed by.

"Valerie. There you are, dear. Your friends were looking all over for you backstage." Emily crossed the short bit of grass and came up to stand beside her.

Valerie had been pressing her back against the warm brick with her face turned up to the sun, and she looked completely exhausted when she opened her eyes to look at Emily. "I'll have to make my apologies. This was a very big morning for me."

"I can see that it was." Emily now knew the heartache the poor girl had gone through. She'd lost her parents, which was a worse tragedy than most people had to go through.

Then, even though she'd found a home with a wealthy aunt who could provide her with everything she needed, she was still trying to find her way in the world.

"I didn't like having to talk about my work at Dress for Success," Valerie continued as she picked an invisible piece of lint off her pantsuit. "Not after what happened to Brianna. I'm pretty sure the judges knew about the murder, but of course they were going to ask me about it anyway. I can't really blame them, since it's a requirement of the program, but it would've been nice if they'd have let me skip it."

Emily wanted to wrap her in a hug. "You did a wonderful job of it, if that makes things any better."

"A little, I suppose. And I guess I did well enough, because I passed this part of the program." Valerie gave her a small smile.

"You did! Oh, that's wonderful! I can't say that I'm surprised, considering the work you did on these ensembles. You're truly a very talented girl." Emily felt a certain sense of pride, even though she hardly knew Valerie.

Valerie's smile increased, although she still looked incredibly tired around the eyes. "Now let's just hope that whatever designer I get to intern under feels the same way. It's going to be a lot of hard work, and I'll constantly have to fight my way to the top, but this is something I'm very serious about."

Serious enough to murder someone who might stand in her way? After all the other hard work she'd done, getting let go from Dress for Success would've probably ruined Valerie's chances of getting the internship. Emily knew that a murder case couldn't simply be solved by gut feelings, but that was what she had to go on when it came to Valerie. She just couldn't convince herself that Valerie had done it, and yet everything always led back to her. "As you should be, considering how good you are. You already know that I'm no fashion expert, but I thoroughly believe in you, Valerie."

"Thank you, and thank you for all that you've done to help me."

"You look like you might want to go home and get some sleep," Emily advised. "This has completely drained you, I think."

Valerie toed a small rock on the pavement. "Some of it is this, yes, but I haven't been sleeping well. I just keep lying awake at night, wondering what happened to Brianna and going through all the possibilities in my mind."

Emily could certainly understand that! She would've liked to tell her that she was on the case and would be sure to get to the bottom of it, but what if she couldn't?

The front doors opened, and Aunt Minnie came charging out of them. Her eagle eyes scanned the parking lot and then swiveled, turning directly toward Valerie. "There you are. I was waiting for you, and I even had to go backstage to look for you. What on earth are you doing standing out here?"

"I'm sorry. I was discussing the show with one of my models," Valerie explained.

"Yes. Right." Minnie strode forward with her hand extended, and several large rings sparkled in the sun. "Minnie Ferguson. Nice to meet you."

"The pleasure is all mine." It certainly wasn't, but this woman didn't look particularly pleased, either. Minnie eyed Emily with all the same disdain she'd shown back at To the Nines, her lip curling up into a sneer.

Minnie patted at her steely gray hair that'd been carefully coifed at the back of her head, though not a strand of it was out of place. "I was surprised that Valerie chose to go with a non-traditional model for this test, and I can't say that I thought it would be a good idea. I suppose I still have to thank you for helping my niece."

That was a very thinly disguised insult at Emily's age and size, she knew, but she wouldn't allow herself to be offended. "I was more than happy to do it, and I appreciate that Valerie allowed me to be a part of her education."

"She did pass, so perhaps it was the particular challenge of trying to make an outfit that actually looked nice with hair that color," Minnie replied, sneering openly at Emily's mop of red curls that'd been pinned into containment for the day.

There were far more people in Emily's life who'd teased her for her hair than she could count, and so Minnie hardly counted at all. "It was indeed a challenge, and one that Valerie easily rose up to."

Valerie's head swiveled on her neck as she watched the two of them like a tennis match. Her tired eyes widened with horror and her cheeks reddened. "Aunt Minnie, it was very kind of Emily to volunteer for me. It's not easy for people to just march out on that stage when they don't have any experience."

It was a very tactful way of avoiding the actual insult while still reprimanding her aunt, and Emily had to give the girl credit for that one.

"Isn't that exactly what I said?" Minnie replied with a smile that didn't even come close to reaching her eyes. "Now, we really must get going. We have so many other things to do today. Come, Valerie."

Valerie's eyebrows lowered as soon as her aunt turned her back, but she didn't argue. "I'm sorry, Emily. I've got to go. I'm sure I'll see you around again sometime soon. Thank you again."

"You're very welcome, dear. Good luck in the next part of your education. I'm sure you'll do wonderfully." Emily watched as Valerie rushed off after Aunt Minnie. A long, dark car had pulled up to the curb, pausing to let them in. It was the same vehicle, Emily noted, as the one she'd seen outside of Dress for Success that day that she and Anita had gone shopping. The driver was different this time, but there couldn't be very many vehicles like that in Little Oakley.

Emily waved as the car pulled away, just in case Valerie could see her. She could just imagine the conversation the two of them were having inside, and she truly hoped Valerie would get the chance to fully appreciate the internship she'd just worked so hard to earn. The girl was sweet and talented, and she deserved to go far.

Minnie, on the other hand, was a viper. It was obvious to Emily that she'd barely restrained herself at all in expressing what she truly thought, and she had a way of lambasting whoever or whatever she wanted without being obvious enough to make them start an argument with her. Valerie definitely didn't have a killer inside of her, but Emily couldn't be too sure about Minnie.

12

"Well, my dear, we've finally got some time to ourselves again." Emily reached into the fridge and found a bottle of wine. "What do you think we should do this evening?"

Rosemary, seeing that Emily wasn't taking anything like tuna out of the fridge, turned toward the living room with her tail in the air.

"Yes, I think you're right. A nice, relaxing evening on the couch would be wonderful." Pouring herself a generous glass, Emily rolled her shoulders as she followed the cat into the next room. She hadn't realized just how tense she'd gotten over the past week as she'd taken on the job at Phoenix Insurance. Sitting at a desk all day wasn't exactly a physically taxing job, but the strain of re-learning something she thought she already knew had clearly gotten to her. Her shoulders had knots in them, and her legs were stiff.

She was also feeling the effects of not getting anything done creatively over the past week. Emily put the glass of wine on the side table and sat down next to Rosemary. "Now then," she said as she picked up her notepad. While Emily would need to type it all up later, she found that writing with a pen and paper was always the best way to get the ideas flowing. "I know I thought of plenty of topics for blog posts this week in regard to finance, so let's see if I can remember them all. Let's start with budgeting. That's my favorite, and I think I could write an article about creating a household budget with my eyes closed."

Rosemary turned in several circles on the couch before settling down with her back pressed against Emily's leg. She pointedly put her fluffy tail over her face and closed her eyes.

"Some help you are," Emily cracked softly as she ran her fingers through the cat's thick fur. "I know. This has been a hard week on you, too. You're used to me being here with you most of the day, and you're always helping me with my blog, or cooking, or crafts. Poor little thing, now that I've run off to earn a paycheck again. Well, maybe if people start liking my financial advice on my blog well enough, it'll keep me from doing that again."

Deep, rumbling purrs emanated from Rosemary as she squeezed her eyes a little tighter.

"Yes, you like that idea, don't you? Let's see what else I could do. I could talk about ways to earn a little bit of extra money on the side when things get tight. I know I don't have a full-time job right now other than taking care of you, Rosemary, but I think working over at Phoenix has been sort of like that. There are all sorts of other options that could come up for people when they need some extra income." She scribbled out the idea on her notepad.

"How about sales?" Emily was on a roll now. "I could do a deep dive on them, explaining how they create an urgency in the buyer to purchase something right away because they believe it won't be available again. Well, either that or the item will never go on such a good discount again. I know that's not true, but people don't think about it when they're at the store."

Thoughts were rolling so quickly through her mind that she was having a hard time keeping up, and Emily was thoroughly enjoying it. This time at Phoenix Insurance had forced her to set her blog aside for the moment, but the break had been good for her. She made notes about creating a budget for the day while shopping, signing up for reward programs at stores but being careful about buying too much just to earn those rewards, and letting your friends know that you're on a budget so that they won't try to influence you to buy that designer skirt.

"I think Valerie could help me out when it comes to clothing," Emily continued, even though Rosemary was thoroughly asleep by this point. "She could help me point out the differences in less expensive clothing versus top label and what people should be looking for in a garment. That might be fun for her, and of course I wouldn't mind seeing her again."

With so many plans ahead of her and her sweet cat beside her, Emily was easily slipping back into the cozy comfort of being at home. She'd been out running around all week, whether she was doing errands, working, having lunch, shopping, or trying to figure out what happened to Brianna. Though her curiosity still niggled at the back of her mind, it was nice to finally let herself relax.

"There now," she said after she had two full pages of notes to go back and look at later. "Why don't we just turn on the evening news and let those ideas simmer for a bit? Who knows? I might even find something else to write about."

Emily clicked on the television, ready to pick up her pen again should the need arise.

"In local stories tonight," the anchor said, staring seriously at the camera, "we were informed two days ago that an arrest had been made in the death of Brianna Hodgkins, but police were keeping the details under wraps while they continued their investigation. Tonight, we're able to tell you that the suspect is Sean Thompson, seen here. While there hasn't been any conclusive evidence made available just yet, it seems that police are still trying to determine the connection this man has to the murder case, if any. Thompson is set to be released on bail tomorrow morning."

"Well, will you look at that!" Emily knew of the arrest, but Alyssa hadn't been able to tell her who it was. She studied the mugshot presented on the screen, and she knew it wasn't Peter or Jonah. He did look familiar, though, and her mind worked hard as she tried to remember if she'd ever seen him before.

"I suppose I could've even passed him in the grocery store," Emily wondered aloud as the news cut to a commercial break. "That's the thing about living in a small town. If there's a killer out there on the streets, I've probably met them before. It doesn't make things any less disturbing, I'll tell you that."

Rosemary, still mostly asleep, stretched out her two front paws and made a tiny squeaky noise in her throat before curling back up.

"Some help you are," Emily chuckled. "I just bore you to death, don't I?"

Emily polished off her glass of wine and carefully got up off the couch, trying not to disturb Rosemary, in order to rinse it out. As she reached the kitchen doorway, she froze. Emily slowly turned around again and stared at the television. The news had come back on, but now they were talking about the weather.

"Bored to death," she murmured. "I know where I saw his face before!"

At her exclamation, Rosemary lifted her head and gave an inquisitive meow.

"Yes! That car that was parked on the street when Anita and I went shopping. We passed by, and I saw the driver. He looked so bored, and I was amused. That was the same man!" Emily flapped her hands in the air for a moment as she tried to decide what to do, and then she patted her pockets in search of her cell phone. They were empty.

"Where did I leave it?" she fretted as she poked her head into the kitchen. She'd been alert and on guard all week as she'd tried to figure this whole thing out, but now that all the clues were fitting together, she hardly knew how to contain herself.

When she finally located her phone in her purse, Emily hesitated. This was going to be a difficult phone call to make, but it had to be done. She dialed Valerie's number.

13

"This is an interesting little piece, and I think it's worth quite a bit more than the tag on it says." Emily turned over the little teapot to check the manufacturer and nodded. "Yes, I think this will be just perfect."

"I didn't know you were in need of a new teapot," Anita commented as she perused a little display of jewelry.

Emily carefully arranged the teapot on a nearby shelf and used her cell phone to take a picture of it. "I don't, but it would be the perfect example for my blog. You see, someone could go out and buy a brand-new item, or they might be able to get the same thing here for a fraction of the price. That can go in the budgeting blog. To further the point, this could be resold for a profit if someone were trying to make a bit of extra cash on the side."

"You've really thought about all this, haven't you?" Anita picked up a vintage brooch in the shape of a flower and held it to the light.

"Absolutely! It took only a small amount of time at Phoenix Insurance to remind me of all the knowledge I'd accumulated over the years. I can't say that it's a topic that'll keep me occupied forever, as I think I'll get tired of lecturing everyone soon enough, but it'll do for the moment. Oh, and the bonus of buying something from here at The Jenkins Foundation is that all the proceeds go toward helping your fellow man. You can't get much better than getting a bargain, potentially turning a profit, and donating to charity all at the same time!" Emily felt a fantastic sense of pride as she moved on to the next display.

"They have some nice clothes here if you still need a thing or two for your wardrobe," Anita noted.

Though she knew there were likely some bargains on the rack, Emily didn't even want to bother looking. "I'm completely done with shopping for clothes, thank you very much! What I bought is more than enough, and most of the time I won't even have an occasion to wear it!"

"Speaking of clothes," Anita began as they stepped back out onto the pavement and headed down the street, "you told me you'd explain all the dirty details today if we went shopping just for fun."

"I did, didn't I?" Emily glanced around, but nobody was near them. "It's kind of wild, really. Valerie's Aunt Minnie understood that Valerie had to have solid work experience in retail clothing for her fashion design program. She might not have been able to wave her checkbook and make all of her niece's problems go away, but she certainly wasn't going to let some girl who refused to work as hard as Valerie ruin her chances at a great career just because she was jealous. She could, however, wave her checkbook at her driver and get him to do a little extra work on the side. He bumped off Brianna before she could cause too much trouble, and then she swapped him out for a different driver just in case anyone had seen him in the area."

"But then how come she didn't just wave her checkbook and make the whole thing go away once the police arrived?" Anita pressed. "I heard there was a confession, and that doesn't sound like the sort of thing a woman like her would do."

"I have to agree. I wasn't sure it would really go anywhere once I understood who was behind it, because I thought for sure her lawyers would manage it for her. Should we grab some coffee to go? I think I could use some extra fuel while we hit the rest of these stores." Emily gestured toward The Daydream Café, a place that was quickly becoming her favorite. She remembered that she'd probably want to stop in at The Dish sometime just to see Jonah and ask him how he was getting along.

When they came back outside, lidded cups in hand, Anita was more than ready for the rest of the story. “Out with it! You’ve kept it to yourself long enough!”

Truthfully, Emily was about ready to burst. “Valerie was the real key. I can’t say that I enjoyed telling her my theory, about how her aunt had manipulated her driver into murdering Brianna. Valerie didn’t particularly like it, either, but she listened to everything I had to say. Then she went straight to Minnie and confronted her with it.”

Anita gasped. “She’s a brave girl!”

“I think so,” Emily agreed. Her coffee was still a bit too hot to drink, but she enjoyed the warmth of it in her hands. “Surprisingly, Minnie admitted everything. I suppose she figured that Valerie would understand why she’d done it. But Valerie has such a sweet nature, she couldn’t let something like that sit on her conscience. I’d given her Alyssa’s number, and she reported the whole thing.”

Poor Valerie. She’d already had everything taken away from her when her parents had passed away. She’d told Emily about the car crash at tea yesterday afternoon. Now, though her aunt had been an integral part of her life, she’d be going away for a long time. Emily had assured her that she was there for her in any capacity that she could be, and Valerie had appreciated it. Fortunately, she hadn’t even been upset with Emily for making what might’ve sounded like wild accusations.

"And what about that?" They were passing To the Nines. The displays and racks inside the store were still full, the clothes hanging and ready until someone decided to unlock the door and turn the lights on once again. A small sign on the door explained that the place would be closed until further notice.

Emily suspected that might be permanent. "Minnie has a way of knowing what people want and what lengths they'll go to in order to get it. You see, Minnie schemed with Melissa to have her gather information about Brianna and Dress for Success. She knew Melissa was already angry with Brianna for leaving her, so it was a simple matter. Melissa was able to tell her of any drama that she heard from Brianna or the rest of the crew, as well as all of their normal comings and goings. Initially, I think Minnie just wanted information about Brianna so she could keep her out of Valerie's way, but it also made it easy for Minnie to tell her driver just how and when to find Brianna when she'd be alone."

"That's rather terrifying," Anita remarked. She blew into her cup and took a careful sip. "Do you think Melissa knew anything about the murder?"

"Not at first." Emily clearly remembered just how distraught Melissa had been when she'd last seen her, as though the information had suddenly come down and hit her like a load of bricks. "It sounds as though Minnie thought she might be able to frame Melissa for the whole deal. Once she realized just how deep she'd gotten, she packed her bags and ran. She's somewhere in the wind now. I just wish I could've stopped her, since she'd have been all right if she'd stayed around here."

"Don't blame yourself for that," Anita advised. "You did everything you could. There's something I don't understand, though."

"What's that?" Emily had gone through the last couple of weeks mostly feeling as though she didn't understand anything at all. Once one clue led to another, she'd often felt like she was looping right back around and starting at the beginning all over again.

"You said Minnie was the snobby lady we met at To the Nines."

"Correct?"

"Then why was she saying such bad things about Dress for Success? Wouldn't she have wanted everyone to shop there so that Valerie would have great work experience?" Anita tucked a bit of her pale blonde hair behind her ear. "It just doesn't make sense."

"I agree, and I've been thinking about that a bit," Emily admitted. "I almost didn't bring it up, since poor Valerie had suffered enough, but I dared to ask her. She explained Minnie's reasoning: If fewer people shopped at Dress for Success, then Peter would have cause to let one of the salesgirls go. The only reasonable choice would be Brianna, since she made far fewer sales and because Peter was terrified of Minnie. Yes, Brianna had accused Valerie of stealing all of those sales, but he probably knew better."

"My goodness." Anita slumped her shoulders as they stepped into a small bookshop. "You certainly got in up to your elbows this time, my dear. It's a good thing you're all done with your job at the insurance company. Or are you?" She raised an eyebrow in challenge.

"Oh, yes!" Emily said as she flopped down onto one of the worn leather chairs in the lobby area of the shop. "Let's see. I retired from my full-time job, but then I went back to work at Pierce's Auto Body for a minute. Now that I went back to Phoenix as well, I suppose that make this my re-re-retirement!"

The two of them shared a laugh that earned them a concerned look from the shop owner behind the counter.

Anita sat down in the chair next to her. "And you already said that you're not going to do finance blogs forever, so what are you going to do with yourself? Other than spoiling Rosemary and spending a hefty amount of your free time with me, of course?"

"Did you miss me?" Emily teased.

"Of course I did," Anita admitted with a smile, "but I know you, and I know you always need to feel like you're doing something. I assume you have some sort of plan for your future."

"Hmm." Emily glanced around. The bookshop was a cozy little place, with a threadbare rug and shelves upon shelves of books. They stretched the entire depth and breadth of the store, and the whole place smelled like old paper. It was comfortable and quiet. "Maybe I'll actually just sit down and read a book or two. I imagine there are all sorts of classics I completely passed by while I was raising my children or working full time, and I think Rosemary would very much appreciate the downtime."

"We'll see if you can actually stick to that plan. I'd be willing to bet money you'll read five pages and then be up and doing something again. You'll end up painting a room or running off to get another job," Anita pointed out.

Emily smiled. She knew Anita was just goading her, but it wasn't without good reason. She did seem to need to keep herself occupied ever since she'd retired from Phoenix Insurance. Even the blog was a way to keep herself busy. "You're not wrong, but I'm still going to prove you wrong. It's about time I actually learned to relax. In fact, I think I'll pick out some books today to get me started."

"Don't you have some at home you haven't read?"

"I do, but there's nothing like a few new ones for inspiration!" Emily got up off the comfy leather chair and headed into the rows of shelves, looking for her next great adventure.

THANK YOU FOR CHOOSING A PUREREAD BOOK!

We hope you enjoyed the story, and as a way to thank you for choosing PureRead we'd like to send you this free Special Edition Cozy, and other fun reader rewards...

Click Here to download your free Cozy Mystery
PureRead.com/cozy

Thanks again for reading.
See you soon!

OTHER BOOKS IN THIS SERIES

If you loved this story and want to follow Emily's antics in other fun easy read mysteries continue **dive straight into other books in this series...**

Read them all...

A Troubling Case Of Murder On The Menu

A Crafty Case Of Murder At The Fair

A Hairy Case of Murder At The Animal Sanctuary

A Clean & Tidy Case of Murder - A Truly Messy Mystery

A Cranky Case of Murder at the Autostore

A Colorful Case of Stolen Art at the Gallery

OUR GIFT TO YOU

AS A WAY TO SAY THANK YOU WE WOULD LOVE TO SEND YOU THIS SPECIAL EDITION COZY MYSTERY FREE OF CHARGE.

Our Reader List is 100% FREE

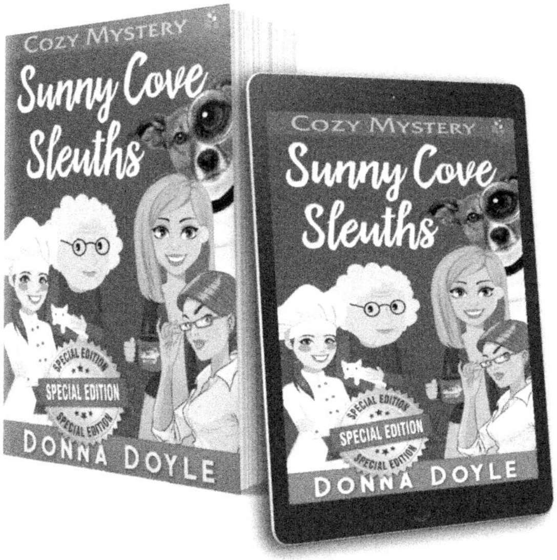

Click Here to download your free Cozy Mystery

PureRead.com/cozy

At PureRead we publish books you can trust. Great tales without smut or swearing, but with all of the mystery and romance you expect from a great story.

Be the first to know when we release new books, take part in our fun competitions, and get surprise free books in your inbox by signing up to our Reader list.

As a thank you you'll receive this exclusive Special Edition Cozy available only to our subscribers...

Click Here to download your free Cozy Mystery

PureRead.com/cozy

Thanks again for reading.

See you soon!

Printed in Great Britain
by Amazon

39795402R10061